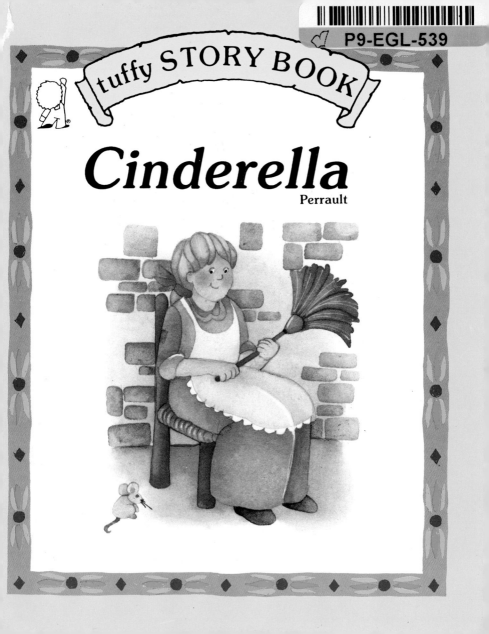

tuffy STORY BOOK

Cinderella
Perrault

Once upon a time there was a little girl who lived with a mean stepmother and two mean stepsisters.

Each day she had to scrub the kitchen and clean the chimney. She was so covered with soot, they called her Cinderella.

One day the king and queen invited all the young girls in their kingdom to an elegant ball. They wanted their son, the prince, to choose a wife.

When an invitation to the ball arrived at Cinderella's house, her stepmother and stepsisters were delighted.

"One of you lucky girls will be the prince's bride," said the stepmother.

They didn't bother to show the invitation to poor Cinderella.

"Why should we?" the sisters said. "She's not nearly as pretty as we are."

Cinderella's sisters spent days preparing for the prince's ball. They worried over which gowns to wear. They wondered which fine jewels to wear. They had many fine things to pick from.

The stepsisters spent hours in front of their mirrors. They changed their outfits over and over. They couldn't even decide on a hair style. Nothing seemed pretty enough.

The sisters treated Cinderella like a maid. They made her wash and iron their clothes, and sew new ones. They didn't even bother to say "Thank you."

The day of the prince's ball arrived at last. The sisters and their mother left Cinderella home alone, sad and lonely.

Cinderella sat by the chimney crying. All of a sudden, a Good Fairy appeared in the window. "Don't cry, Cinderella," she said.

"Would you like to go to the ball?" the Good Fairy asked.

"Oh, yes!" Cinderella said. "But I have no pretty clothes to wear, or a fine carriage to ride in."

"We'll see about that," the Good Fairy said. "Bring me a pumpkin."

Cinderella ran to the garden. The Good Fairy tapped six little mice with her wand. They changed into six fine horses.

"There are your horses," said the Good Fairy when Cinderella returned with a bright orange pumpkin. "Now put that on the ground and you shall have an elegant coach, too"

With a touch of her wand, the Good Fairy changed the pumpkin into a beautiful golden carriage.

She changed Cinderella's rags into a beautiful gown. And a rat scurrying past was changed into a footman to drive the carriage.

"Now you have everything you need to attend the prince's ball," said the Good Fairy. "A coach and footman, six horses, and a gown fit for a princess."

Then the Good Fairy looked Cinderella straight in the eye. "But remember this. You must leave the ball before the palace clock strikes midnight."

Six galloping horses carried
Cinderella to the royal palace.
The prince turned as she
entered. "She's the loveliest of
them all," he whispered.

Captivated by her beauty, the
prince asked Cinderella to dance
with him.

The happy prince didn't leave Cinderella's side all evening. He danced every dance with her.

Cinderella's stepsisters watched with envy. They didn't realize the beautiful girl was the girl they treated so badly.

Cinderella was so happy she forgot about the time.

Suddenly the big palace clock began to strike midnight.

Cinderella remembered the Good Fairy's warning. She raced from the palace.

As she ran down the palace steps, one of her tiny glass slippers fell off.

The prince chased after Cinderella, but she was gone. He spied the glass slipper and knew at once it was hers. He picked it up tenderly.

The clock struck twelve just as Cinderella's coach reached home. It instantly turned back into a pumpkin. The footman was changed back into a rat. And the six horses scurried away as tiny mice again.

Many days passed. The prince could not forget the beautiful girl from the ball. Every time he looked at the glass slipper he thought of her.

At last the king and queen decided to search for the shoe's owner. They announced that the prince would marry the girl who could wear the tiny glass slipper.

Cinderella's stepsisters tried to put on the slipper but their feet were much too big.

The prime minister had already visited every house in the land trying to find who owned the glass slipper. As he was leaving Cinderella's house, he noticed her sitting in a corner.

"Aren't you going to try to put on the glass slipper?" asked the Prime minister.

Cinderella's stepsisters roared with laughter. "Her!" they said. "Why, she's just a kitchen maid. Whatever makes you think she could wear it?"

But to everyone's surprise, Cinderella's foot fit perfectly into the tiny glass slipper.

The prince married Cinderella. The new princess, as good as she was beautiful, forgave her stepmother and stepsisters. She invited them to live in the palace. They all lived happily ever after.